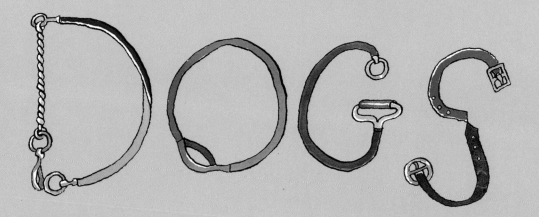

DOGS

ARE MY FAVORITE THINGS

With love and thanks to Margaret—J.H.

For Holly, with love—M.C.

This edition first published in the United States in 2002 by MONDO Publishing, by arrangement with
The Bodley Head Children's Books, Random House, 20 Vauxhall Bridge Road, London, SW1V 2SA.
Text copyright © 2001 by Judy Hindley. Illustrations copyright © 2001 by Margaret Chamberlain.

For information contact:
MONDO Publishing
980 Avenue of the Americas
New York, NY 10018
Visit our web site at http://www.mondopub.com

Printed in Hong Kong
First MONDO printing 2002
ISBN 1-59034-035-3
02 03 04 05 06 07 08   9 8 7 6 5 4 3 2 1

Originally published in London in 2001 by The Bodley Head Children's Books.

DOGS

ARE MY FAVORITE THINGS

by Judy Hindley and Margaret Chamberlain

MONDO

Wherever I go,
I look for dogs.
Dogs are my favorite things.

Big dogs,

small dogs,

long dogs,

tall dogs,

any dogs, and
all dogs.

2

Do you like them, too?

I love every single kind of dog.

Slick, neat show dogs,   and very old slow dogs.

Dogs that work,   and dogs that play.

4

Dogs that just sit around all day.

Dogs that waddle,

and dogs that race!

Dogs with a little, flat, squashed-up face.

Dogs with little pointy ears
that twitch at every sound.

Dogs with flippy-floppy ears
that almost touch the ground.

A bulldog,

a beagle,

a poodle,

and a pug.

A big, sleepy sheepy dog.

A dog that's like a rug.

I don't care what kind it is,
as long as it's a dog!

Dogs in a shop,

dogs in a park,

dogs in a house,

and dogs in the dark.

Dogs in a group,
dogs in a crowd,

dogs that are gentle,
and dogs that are loud.

11

Barking dogs,

playing dogs,

walking dogs,

NO DOGS

and talking dogs!

White dogs,

brown dogs,

yellow dogs,

and clown dogs.

Tall, slim, spotty dogs,
snotty dogs,
dotty dogs,
goony, loony, crazy dogs!
Fat dogs and lazy dogs.

Freckled, speckled, dotted dogs,
knotted dogs, and spotted dogs.
Slim, lean, bare dogs,

HUGE
DOGS,

square dogs,

hairy dogs,

scary dogs,

bouncy little merry dogs,

dogs that hunt,   dogs that herd,

and dogs that howl at the moon:

AROOO!

I really do like all of them!

But . . .

. . . one of them would do!